THIS BOOK BELONGS TO

_____

Marshall had been doing exercises in front of the Lookout all week. He was training for the Fastest Fire Pup Trophy!

"Hose out!" barked Marshall, taking aim. He shot water from the hose and straight into a bucket. "I did it!"

The other pups cheered him on.

Next, he had to perform a rescue. He drove his fire truck to a tree where Cali waited.

But the ladder hit the tree and broke. Then, Marshall fell with a BUMP!

I'M OKAY!

Ryder watched from the Lookout.

"It looks like Marshall could use a helping hand," he said, pushing a button on the PupPad.

"PAW Patrol to the Lookout!"

And with that, all the Pup Tags lit up and the team raced to the tower.

In the control room, the pups lined up, ready for action.

"This time, Marshall is the emergency. He needs our help," said Ryder. "But we just want you to do your best and not worry about whether you break the record."

"Do my best and forget the rest," said Marshall.

"Rocky, I need you to find something in your recycling truck to fix Marshall's ladder," said Ryder.

"Don't lose it, reuse it!" Rocky said.

The pups raced out of the Lookout.

Outside, Rocky rummaged in his truck, looking for something to fix the ladder.

ROCKY TO THE RESCUE!

"This broom will work," barked Rocky. "I'll use the handle to make new rungs for your fire ladder, Marshall."

Rocky screwed the new rungs into place.

Ryder received a call.
It was Mayor Goodway!

"There's a TV crew waiting
to film Marshall break the
Fastest Fire Pup record," she
said. "He's late!"

"Marshall's ready to go," Ryder assured the mayor.

I'M FIRED UP!

The PAW Patrol had to get Marshall
to the starting line right away.

Chase turned on his siren and used his traffic cones to clear the roads.

"My cones will stop the traffic until Marshall gets through," said Chase.

As soon as Marshall arrived at the park, the crew turned on their cameras.

"You're on in three... two... one..." said the cameraman.

"Today, Marshall the Fire Pup will attempt to win the trophy for completing the Fire Rescue Course in the fastest time ever," said Mayor Goodway.

The crowd went wild!

"If Marshall can ring the City Hall bell in less than ten minutes," the mayor continued, "he'll be the Fastest Fire Pup ever! Go!"

Marshall started the race. "Do my best and forget the rest!" he said to himself.

First, he completed the obstacle course. Then, he used his ladder. With the new rungs, Marshall easily climbed up to the tree and rescued the toy cat.

Marshall raced his fire truck to the beach to complete the next task!

"Hose out!" barked Marshall. He took aim and a stream of water put out a fake campfire.

Everyone cheered!

"I did it!" said Marshall. "Now I just have to get to City Hall and ring the bell."

But just as Marshall was about to get in his truck, he spotted a fire . . . a *real* fire!

"I'll take care of that!" barked Marshall. "Hose on!"

Marshall put out the fire with his Pup Pack hose! Hooray!

Everyone cheered for Marshall — especially the mayor!

"You've got thirty seconds left," said Ryder.
"Give it your best!"

Marshall zoomed to City Hall, raced up his ladder to the bell tower, and rang the bell.

DONG!

But he was one minute late! Marshall wasn't the fastest fire pup.

But Mayor Goodway was proud of him. "You stopped to put out a *real* fire and that makes you an Adventure Bay hero!"

She presented Marshall with the trophy. "This trophy is now . . ." she said, "for the *Greatest* Fire Pup in the World!"

And everyone cheered!

Later, back at the Lookout, the PAW Patrol watched Marshall on the news.

"You did it, Marshall!" the pups shouted.

"I really did do my best!" he said.